WINDOWS

MARCUS BLAKE

~ THE MARCUS BLAKE COLLECTION ~

WINDOWS

A Mavericknes Media / Truesource Publishing book

WINDOWS was edited by
Carol Felder and J M Almgreen

The story is fictional and any resemblance to actual
people, places, and certain facts associated with the
characters created by Marcus Blake is purely
coincidence.

Mavericknes Media : Dallas Texas

Truesource Publishing : Dallas Texas

www.truesourcepublishing.com

ISBN : 978-1-932996-65-4

Printed in the United States of America
Published in Dallas, Texas

For More information on Marcus Blake go to....

www.marcusblake.net
www.facebook.com/themarcusblake
www.twitter.com/marcusblake
www.thatnerdshow.com

About the Author

     Marcus Blake was born in Chicago, Illinois in 1977. He grew up in Chicago and East Texas. His education is in History, Literature, Psychology, and Religion & Philosophy. Marcus Blake has studied at many universities throughout the United States, but his Alma Mater is Stephen F. Austin State University in Nacogdoches, Texas, which is also where he wrote his first book, The Music of Life. Marcus Blake is a Poet, Musician, Comedian, Writer, and Historian. His books are The Music of Life, My Reflections, Returning Home. Sex Game. The Lonely Girl, Stories From Wrigley, 30 Minutes: Trust and Lies, 30 Minutes: Guilty Until Proven Innocent, 30 Minutes: A Soldier's Song, and 30 Minutes: A Badge of Honor. . He has taught in the public school system, served in the Army, and been a guest speaker at Education and Literary events throughout the world. Marcus Blake is also a Radio Host, his current show is Saturday Morning Nerd Show which can be heard on Saturday Mornings at www.thatnerdshow.com. He is a veteran of Rock and Roll shows as well as Political shows on the radio. Marcus Blake makes his home in the Dallas, Texas.

OTHER BOOKS BY MARCUS BLAKE...

The Music of Life

My Reflections

Returning Home

Sex Game

The Lonely Girl

Stories From Wrigley

30 Minutes: Trust and Lies

30 Minutes: Guilty Until Proven Innocent

30 Minutes: A Soldier's Song

30 Minutes: A Badge of Honor

Ring of Warriors: Making a Fighter

To First Loves

1

If I have learned anything about Love, it doesn't have one definition. It's defined by many things because it means something different for each one of us. For me it has always been finding my way back to something I have always known...a truth that I tried to ignore, but just couldn't. Yeah, it may not make much sense, but then again, you have to know my story. And today, I would be reminded once again.

Looking out the window from my office, I could see that the day was starting out cloudy with the sun slowly peeking out from behind; it was days like this that always let me know it was going to be a long day for me, but I didn't know if that was going to be a bad thing or a good thing, yet I hoped that it would turn out to be a good thing, but only time could tell. The city of Denver, where I lived, was buzzing with all sorts of excitement. Ski season was in full force now and all the resorts near the city had just received some really good snow.

Thanksgiving was a couple days away, which brought the usual tourists and ski bums to all the surrounding Denver areas. It also didn't hurt that Christmas was only a month away, which seemed to be everybody's favorite holiday or at least everybody that I knew. Also, John Elway and the Broncos were on their way to their second straight Super Bowl; life couldn't get much better than that! It was exciting times right now, especially at the radio station that I work at.

My name is Blake Conrad and I'm a radio DJ for a classic rock station, although it seems to be more of a political satire station with all the lampooning that we do of the local and national politicians. We do spend a lot of our air time humorously talking about Colorado and American politics with a few satirical interviews of politicians trying to get their message out to the people anyway they can. Most of the time, it gives me great pleasure to be funny with some of these clowns.

Although, sometimes we get a few politicians that seem to mean what they say and are inspiring to talk to, but anyone who listens to my show knows that I am just kidding. I have a great job. I get to listen to great music, and can honestly say that I am perfectly happy. How many people can really say that. Though, it was not always this way because to have a perfectly content and happy life usually means one had to struggle and sacrifice to get to that point.

Every thanksgiving the station has people write in and say what they are thankful for and how they are blessed in their sometimes monotonous lives. We will pick what we think are the most heart-felt to read on the air. This is our way of trying to make our listeners feel good during the holidays.

This week I was showing a new DJ the ropes and he asked me what was the best "Thankful Notes" as we like to call them, I'd ever read on the air. It didn't take me long to think of that one special note that really meant something to me. Actually to be honest, it was my own, my own personal love story. I have been married for about three years now with my first child on the way, but the road that my wife and I traveled to get to that point was a long, emotionally, hard fought battle.

Joe, the new guy I was training at the end of the day asked me. "Well, what is this great love story of yours that I keep hearing about because you know I really could use a good story these days with all the trouble I am having with my girlfriend."

I looked at him sharply and said. "Let me guess, she wants to get married, but you can't seem to figure out if you love her enough to marry her."

He just chuckled and answered. "How did you know, is it that obvious?"

I replied. "Mister, the one thing I absolutely know is that you will never know how much she has meant to you until she's gone. Sounds like a cliché I know, but it's true." Joe looked puzzled, but I knew that he needed to hear my story. Sometimes all we need is a good story to help see the light at the end of the tunnel. I told him that I would explain what I meant over a couple of drinks after work courtesy of the station we were employed at. It could be a working dinner.

About 7:30 that night, Joe, my boss Steve, and I arrived at a little local jazz bar called Uncle Charlie's, a place where we usually went to because of the music and the free drinks. They liked our station and promoted the club so it was a win, win. It was piano night so we were treated to some of the local jazz pianists. Steve and I had known each other for a lot of years, ever since our days at the University of Colorado, where we both were English and Communication Majors. I was the true

Literary fan, he only got the English degree, so he could kept having classes with a girl he liked. It worked because he ended up marrying her.

Although, he decided to stay within the business side of radio, I found that my talent was on the air. I looked at Joe and said to him. "Hope you did not have to be somewhere tonight because this story is a long one, but a funny one and worth hearing; just ask Steve."

Steve spoke up. "Joe, I have heard a lot of crazy stories, some very heartfelt and some that were just stupid because of the people involved, but I have never known a story that you can get so much inspiration from and learn what not to do. If you are having trouble with your girlfriend then is a good story to hear." It was always nice to get his seal of approval.

I gave Joe a serious look. "The one thing you need to understand about this story is that you have to hear it from the beginning, the best stories almost always start at the beginning. " And then I proceeded to tell this long and complicated story, the one that seemed to sum up my

life to this point. It all started my first year
of college.

2

I was from a little Michigan town called South Haven. It was a Lake Michigan coastal town that always had too many tourists in the summer and never enough going on in the winter, but it was still a very beautiful place. More importantly, it was home.

When I was eighteen and had graduated from high school,. I picked a college that was over a thousand miles away; it was the first one that offered me a Football Scholarship and a Music Scholarship. It was an odd combination, but a good education for how life really worked. Believe it or not there are a lot of great life lessons in football and music. I had never heard of this school until I was driving through Kansas during Spring break my senior year. It was a place right in the middle of the state. It was small, but offered a pretty good education. I spent a day there, tried out for the football team as a Quarterback, and after that they offered me a scholarship.

To be honest, I was only rebelling against my parents and just wanted to get as far away as I could.   I had never been to Kansas before…only heard about in history books and one very important classic movie. But I quickly learned that there were no yellow brick roads in Kansas… far from it, A week after graduation, I headed on out of Michigan and never looked back. I went to college a little early so I could do my freshman orientation, take some summer classes, and train for college football. I wasn't a great quarterback in high school, but I was a capable one.

My claim to fame was the fact that I was a smart football player and understood the game from a strategic point of view. I was not going to some big NCAA division 1 school, but a place where I could still play ball, which is all that I really cared about. At the end of the summer more freshmen started to come in, but I didn't get a chance to really meet anybody except my fellow teammates because we were in the middle of three-a-day practices.

After early football practice ended, I started to meet more people, especially girls, and there were a lot of pretty ones. I never thought of Kansas as having pretty girls, a stereotype that couldn't have been more wrong. I guess it had something to do with all the hearty farm girls who proved that curves made women beautiful. Even, though I don't remember too much about what happened that year of my life I can still remember plain as day the first moment I met Kelly.

I was coming out of a team meeting about 10:00 pm one night and she was sitting with a couple of her friends by the campus clock which was in the very center of the campus. Everybody went there to talk or "make-out" because the night sky was never more clear at any other place on campus. This clock was also great because when there was a full moon the moonlight shined brighter in that one spot on campus. And the clock always seemed to be lighting the way for star crossed lovers who dared to cross its threshold.

It was called "Lover's Point" because people would get engaged there; sometimes stay there and kiss all night long, and there had even been a few children conceived there. Anyway, I was tired and going back to the athletic dorm to go to bed when I saw some people there, but I walked past without even saying hello. I was too tired to meet anyone else, but not too tired to see how beautiful she was. Something tells me, that I could never miss her beauty.

As I walked past them, I had noticed her looking back at me when I was staring at her, but I didn't say anything to her or her friends. When I walked past this voice said to me in a very sarcastic way. "Well, some people here just don't have any manners; I thought everybody around here was nice."

I laughed at the memory. And then I continued. "Joe, I turned around to be the biggest, smartest - ass to her that I could be and when I saw her the words were just gone. It was like staring at the face of an angel; she was that beautiful and I was in complete awe for the next few moments. I think I even lost track of time when I stared at her. "

Joe looked at me amused and said. "So basically you made a complete fool of yourself in front of her."

I looked at him with a big smile. "Hell, yes, I embarrassed myself in front of her, but she thought it was completely charming. I literally fell in love with her the first moment I saw her and I'm certain of that now even if I did not see it then. I know that it sounds like nonsense, but it's absolutely true."

After my huge embarrassing moment, I stayed and talked with her and her friends for a few hours. The two friends that were there were actually a couple of her roommates that she had met a few days before. Her new roommates decided about 1:00 am that it was too late and went back to their dorm to sleep, but when it seemed that we would all part company for the evening Kelly and I stayed and talked for another two hours. It was a conversation that I couldn't seem to escape and I was glad not to.

We found out everything about each other that night or at least it seemed like it. She was from a semi - small town in Kansas called Hutchison and a pretty normal background unlike me. Kelly's parents had been married for 25 years and she had a younger brother and sister; she was also very family-oriented. My parents had been divorced since I was a child, to which they had spent the years since they got divorced, fighting and trying to get back at each other through me for the hurt they had caused each other.

In addition, I had a half-sister that was ten years younger than me, to which I didn't know because I never grew up with her. The only oriented type of family I had was with my grandparents who had been married for 50 years. We came from different worlds and really had nothing in common, but we were absolutely crazy for each other. It didn't take long for that to happen. Just like that it happened. Something like out of a Cary Grant movie.

To this day, neither of us can explain it, but we couldn't break the connection between us.

Eventually we had to go back to our dorms and get some sleep. For me, it was hard, all I could be thing think about her. She was something else and I never met a girl like her in high school. I didn't even know there were girls like her when I was in high school. We still had a couple of days before class started so the campus was full of activities for students to get to know each other. I didn't care. I only wanted to see her.

The dorm she lived in was unique. They had these huge windows with a sitting area inside just outside the window. During the reasonably warm days most of the windows stayed open so the Kansas winds would blow light breezes inside the room. The windows were perfect for reading. Perfect sunlight during the day and at night the moonlight shined through the window. If you walked past the girls down on your way to class, you usually saw most them sitting by their window drinking coffee. It was like something

Hemingway would have described about Paris in A Movable Feast.

I found where she lived and went by. Or at least tried to. I was so nervous, I kept walking by the dorm and after the fourth time, I was starting to look like a crazed stalker. Finally a girl passing by sarcastically said to me…"Whoever, you're looking for. Why don't find the courage to go say hi." I was shocked by what she said. But she was profoundly right. I walked past Kelly's window and there she was drinking coffee and reading a book. It was a beautiful sight. If I were a painter, it would have been the perfect scene to paint. My words were hard to find, but she saved me. She looked up and said. "It's about time. I was wondering if you would ever find me again."

I smiled and replied. "Do you believe in fate?"

She looked surprised. "Wow, is that your best line?"

I laughed. "I didn't mean as a line."

"Why not, it's a good one. It would make me pay attention to you."

"I was only curious if you do because I couldn't stop thinking about you."

She just laughed and she had a beautiful laugh. "I couldn't stop thinking of you too."

"Then maybe it is fate."

"Maybe...I guess time will tell."

So there we were. We picked up right where we left off as I sat outside her window. We talked for hours. I almost started quoting something from Romeo and Juliet... after all her face looked stunning in the sunlight, making me think that she just might be the sun in some Shakespearean way. The only true thing I found out that day was, I never wanted our conversation to end. I just wanted to be a part of it, no matter what.

Kelly and I started to date each other that week and being on a small campus, everybody that we knew from the football team to the drama department, which she was very involved in, including the coaches and the professors would give us a hard time about it. Kelly was there at the University on a Music and Drama Scholarship.

She was a great actress and not too shabby of a singer and sax player. I also sang in the choir just to get a little more money for my tuition and it got to be one more class we had together as well as getting to have a lot of fun together with music. Sometimes, it was the only thing that we had in common even though we did not like the same kind; she liked country and I was a classic rock and roll, jazz, and blues man. We really did have a lot of fun during our first semester at college. I was playing college football and having a tremendous time doing it. She was taking part in everything she could when it came to acting in the Drama Department.

That first semester, Kelly was in a couple of plays and the fall musical; she was really fantastic at it even though she did not think so. She was always there every Saturday at the football games and even a few away games cheering us on.

We lived kind of a fairy tale life because it seemed that nothing could ruin it for us, but like all great moments, tragedy hits just to test how great things really are. Unfortunately, we fell victim to that and things between us were not so good in the months that followed. We both had a grandparent that we were very close to pass away without each of us being there.

Since I was a third-string quarterback and on the scout team, I started to get concussions in practice. They resulted in a couple of trips to the hospital and caused a lot of hostility on my part while I was suffering through all the symptoms of having a concussion. It was mainly having migraine headaches all the time, blurred vision, and being subject to blacking out sometimes.

The injuries took their toll on me and I wasn't an easy person to be around. It wasn't hard for me to find myself in a bad mood. Also, it didn't help that I was very much ill-tempered in my youth and that Kelly and I spent most of our time together. Unfortunately she saw my bad side and I saw her as well. Stress and her own misfortunes could cause her emotions to be very unpredictable, which caused a lot of tension between us at times.

To give you an idea about how things could be, one evening we were in the library together studying and I had been teasing her and flirting with her all night like I usually did. She had been joking with me as well and everything was fine with us; we were really happy, at least for the moment. Anyway, a friend of mine came by our table and started to give us a hard time about the fact that we were already married; we just hadn't had a formal wedding yet.

Most of the time I would have just laughed it off because we did act like a married couple on campus, but as soon as he left I started poking fun at him behind his back. Kelly looked at me and said. "Sometimes, you can just be a real jerk towards other people; I don't even know why I put up with you, especially when there are too many guys around here that want to date me."

Well, this made me even angrier because I knew she was right; there were too many other guys that were jealous of me and wanted to be her boyfriend. Instead of admitting that to her and admitting my faults I just looked at her with an angry look and said. "Well, who's stopping you; if want to date other guys then get your ass out of here and do it."

She angrily, but sarcastically said to me. "You think you're a regular Don Juan around here do you, hell a baboon in heat is more of a turn-on than you."

Well, we just went at each other's throats right there in the library; it was so bad that we were kicked out of it and not allowed to be in the library together for the rest of the semester. Although, we did provide some good entertainment for everybody on the campus; it was like the honeymooners in Kansas.

For a while there people would comment that we should just set up a boxing ring, strap on the gloves and go at it; it would have been a harsh marriage like therapeutic tool, but it probably would have been effective for us. It was at that point that I got very serious with Joe and my story turned from just pure entertainment to a lesson on love and life. "Let me ask you, Joe, do you and your girlfriend have a lot of baggage within your relationship" I replied.

Joe replied. "What do you mean, I don't quite understand?

"Well, in all relationships people bring outside problems to them and they can be anything from your family and family history to the major issues that plague your life in the present" I replied back.

He simply answered. "I guess my girlfriend and I have our fair share of problems in each of our lives that were there in the beginning."

I looked at Joe like a schoolteacher would look at their students and said to him. "If we bring our own issues to the relationship, it always hinders the relationship and it becomes a contest just to rise above them and make your relationship succeed."

3

We had only scratched the surface of this story. It was still too early before we got to the good part. I looked at my audience like an English Professor and continued. "Most couples that you see whether they are married or just dating can never rise above them, and in the end they just destroy what they have. Sometimes it can simply be the issue of honesty and if the couple cannot be honest with one another, they will never be able to tell each other how they really feel or what they really want. In the beginning with Kelly and I, being young adults, all the baggage that each of us carried deeply affected our relationship as well as all the problems we were having at that point in our lives. We were two people with serious emotional issues and it became too hard to have some easy-going relationship that didn't cause hardships. It also didn't help that we didn't know how to deal with those problems except through anger; that tends to happen when two stubborn people get together especially when they're young. "

I casually smiled at Joe. "This is why when we first met we didn't build a solid foundation for our union so it would stand strong; part of it, too, was the fact that we were also young and a littlebit foolish. When w young, we don't usually understand any of this until you have made those mistakes within a relationship."

Joe looked at me and jokingly said. "Wow, that's a very profound thing to say about relationships, but I guess it does make sense"

"This is a philosophical way of looking at how relationships can last, but part of it is also having the maturity to recognize the many truths within your relationships. That maturity is also very hard to come by especially when one is still an adolescent; some people claim to live and learn, but I prefer to love and learn."

Like many things in life, love is a continual learning process that just doesn't stop when one gets married, but continues all the days of your life? I just wish I knew all this back then and could have avoided a lot of my mistakes, but if we don't go through those bad times at least once, then we never learn." I continued in teacher's tone and said to my captive audience. "We must always realize this about love and life; we will always have something to learn about love."

We all ordered another round of drinks from the cocktail waitress and I continued my story with them. The piano player was playing a soft Harry Connick Jr. tune and it placed me into a solemn mood as I told this particular part of the story.

By the time the football season had ended that year I was already angry most of the time and distraught over a few things. Kelly was not speaking to me as we left for the Thanksgiving holidays. I didn't go home to see my family like she did and even though we were almost broken up from each other, which we got to that point many times, we just couldn't seem to do it. I didn't want to be anywhere unless she was there.

When everybody returned for the rest of the fall semester we continued not to speak to each other except for the last two days of final's week. The night before everybody was to leave for the Christmas break, I cooked dinner for her and all her roommates as a way of saying I was sorry. We had a great evening and really loved each other that night as two people could without having sex. That night only confirmed for me how much I wanted her to be a part of my life. I was only nineteen years old and looking back it seemed like I was more sure of things back then. I knew what I wanted without any doubts. I can't say that now. We get more cynical as get older. As irony would have it that would also be the last great evening we would have, for a very long time. Even the best love affairs don't always last.

The spring semester was very busy for both of us and we didn't see much of each other. I could tell we were growing apart and finding other things besides each other to fill our needs. The few nights we could see each other usually turned out to be hurtful debates; most of the time about stupid things. We cared more about being right than we did with being with each other and so it was a continual contest just to one up each other.

Kelly was a very stubborn person just like me and I was usually a jerk most of the time because I was still suffering from the symptoms of concussions. It's no excuse for being a jerk, but one should know what was happening to know the whole story, One weekend after getting to see one another only once during the week we got into a fight because I had not shaved for a couple of days and she said she would not have anything to do with me until I did. It was stupid really, but aren't most fights!

Well, I knew she was sort of joking, but at the same time she was a little serious because she hated facial hair. Even though I didn't really have any right to be mad because it wasn't that big of a deal to begin with, I flew off the handle about the issue. I rebelled against her and grew a scruffy beard, and she stood her ground. She would not have any contact with me until I shaved it.

We confirmed yet again to everyone on campus that we were just like a married couple. The funny thing about the issue was that all my football buddies did the same thing; they grew beards and rebelled against their girlfriends. We just wanted to prove that we were in control of our own relationships and that women couldn't control us. We didn't last a month before we were all shaving the beards off. I prefer to think that it proved how much trouble women could be and what men would do not to be lonely instead of losing a battle. And yet, again, I was still wrong.

Also, during the Spring Semester a lot of things happened to us that would change our perspective on life. After a car accident, where it was determined that I had "blacked-out" while driving, caused a trip to the hospital. After that I was forced to give up playing football. A neurologist finally convinced me that I wasn't well enough to keep playing and it would be too dangerous taking any more hits to the head.

When I was faced with the possibility that I could actually die if I took one more serious hit to the head. I knew that it was time to move on. Sometimes dealing with having to give up something you love so much causes the most awful depression. Football had always been a way of dealing with my parent's divorce and something that was very much a part of my life. It was hard to walk away from the game and every athlete, no matter what level they have competed at knows that hurt; sometimes it can be too much trying to cope with the loss.

What most people do is find some other avenue for dealing with that pain. For me, I dealt with it through alcohol and it made it worse because Kelly and I were not dating anymore. For the rest of the Spring Semester it, wasn't very often that I was actually sober.

Kelly was going through some rough times herself. Her family was falling apart and she had two grandparents that she was very close to die that year. Although ,she did not turn to alcohol or drugs to cope with her problems she immersed herself into acting and her classes. Between the plays she was doing on campus every few weeks and her schoolwork she became very stressed out even to the point of going to the hospital for extreme exhaustion.

She was sent home after one night and told to get two weeks of bed rest without doing any work. Joe looked at me with a concerned look. "Did you and Kelly have any more good times with each other that year or was it pretty much the end of it between you and her."

I paused and sorrow draped over my face. . "Yes, there was one other night that we had which was good. We were babysitting that night; one of her roommates took care of this three year old little boy most of the week because his mother worked two jobs and his father wasn't around."

I continued along with the story. "This little boy would actually hang out with Kelly, her other roommates, and I because we were all such a close -knit group. Anyway, that night there was a showing of *The Little Mermaid* on campus for students so we took the kid to go see it and later just hung -out for the rest of the night at her dorm playing with him until his mother came. I don't know why because I never liked children that much, but the kid took a liking to me so he would hang out with me in the guy's athletic dorm sometimes. He learned a lot of different things from my fellow football players! Some of them, not always good."

After stopping for a moment and laughing at the memory, I continued again in my narrative. "Well, that night ended early for us; we hadn't really engaged in that much conversation because there were things still clouding our relationship and what was left of our friendship. What made it a good night was that I realized how truly beautiful she was and I mean that in a maternal sense. The way she was with children as a good mother would be made her even more radiant. When one looks upon a woman and sees that maternal part in her, it is like looking upon the very face of God; it's truly a beautiful sight. It is the same beauty that lies within seeing a mother and newborn child or looking at a painting by Botticelli or Michelangelo. There is just something about it and there is not any other way to describe it; seeing Kelly with a child just made me love her even more and I imagined what it would be like If we had children together.   It's the funny... because until last year I never wanted to have children."

The night was winding down at the club as they did last call, but no one wanted to go. Joe was too curious about how the story ended and was determined to hear it all, even if it took all night. Like all good stories this one was filled with tragedy as well; usually a happiness that comes to an end and a sacrifice that has to be made. We finished our drinks and I continued to tell my story.

The spring semester was winding down and Kelly stayed busy through it and didn't socialize much anymore. We had never officially broken up. We had never had the heart to heart talk except to say that it would be okay if we saw other people. I don't know if we really wanted it to end and by saying it out loud would just make it official. If we did, it would have been too real. So we went through the emotions and saw other people. When she did, she would go out with another guy or be with her best friends. I continued to be depressed and be drunk most of the time. The funny thing is, the times that I was sober was when I was around the kid or spending an evening with Kelly. The Kid turned out to be more of a blessing to me than anything that semester because around him I was at my best which still wasn't all that great to begin with, but better than when I was drinking.

As the year came to a close I didn't socialize with anybody much anymore and seeing the kid came less and less. About a month before school was over Kelly and I spoke our last words to each other. I just didn't know at the time or I would have chosen my words more carefully. I would have said something better.

4

By the time I got this part of the story Joe, Steve, and I had decided to get some breakfast at an IHOP down the street. The sky was still filled with clouds so we couldn't even see the moon or the stars. It was pretty dark in the part of town that we were, but the darkness fit mood of this particular part of the story. As we walked down the street it seemed forever was stalking us, but I continued on with my sad tale.

Kelly was in one of the spring plays and I was supposed to go see her in it because I had promised to be there. Anyway, on the night of the last show we were mad at each other and hadn't said anything nice to each other in a quite a while so I skipped out. I went with some of my friends to a bar to watch the last NBA regular season game and get drunk. When I finally got back, I ran into her at my dorm because she had been visiting a friend. Well, we had the biggest fight that we had ever had right there in the front entrance. That's the night it would finally end...for good.

Kelly with the coldest look I had ever seen, bitterly said to me, "thanks for the support I guess you can't even keep a promise anymore, not that it really matters to you; I can't go through the motions anymore. Blake, I don't ever want to see you again or ever talk to you; you're too much of a drunk. I can't have anything to do with that."

The words pierced my heart like a sword from some old fashion knight and even though I knew she was right, I didn't know how to display anything but anger towards her. I told her that she was a conceited bitch and too self-involved to care about anybody else, but herself. I even went as far as to say that it was only through acting that she could display compassion and that I never really cared about her at all, which was about the biggest lie I had ever told. The thing is she was the most compassionate person that her friends and I had ever known. But I needed her to hurt. I needed to get back at her in some way and that was my way of sticking a knife in her and twisting it deep.

She was willing to help anybody, was always there to listen and try and solve your problems, and more importantly she was a friend to anybody who needed it. I also was very much madly in love with her and despite the drunken states I was usually in I knew that I loved her. Well, after a brief yelling match mainly from me she stormed out. I didn't see her, nor talk to her for the last week of the semester. If I saw her she wouldn't even look at me. If she walked past me, it would be like a cold breeze as if I didn't exist.

We had tried for those last few months of the year to have some kind of relationship, although it never worked. Unfortunately, most of what I said to her that night was the alcohol talking and I didn't realize how much our fight was going to hurt inside till the next day. I thought my headache would be the worst part of my hangover, but it was the heartache that became the worst part.

We did our best to avoid each other for the last week of school. Kelly and I would hear things about each other through friends, but I'm sure the feeling was mutual at the time in that we just didn't care about each other anymore. At least we were not going to admit out loud to anyone. And that is the way we left until the end of the year.

Since we were not speaking, we took different dates to the formal dance the university had every spring at the end of the school year. . While we were there she stayed on one side of the room and I spent most of my time at the bar. We did however spend the evening looking at each other from across the room wondering if one of us was going to say something to the other, but our stubbornness prevailed and we never did.

My date really didn't have that good of a time and it was mainly me she was upset with. If Kelly actually had a good time with the guy she was with I certainly didn't know about it because I was too drunk at the time. When everybody was leaving during final's week Kelly and I stayed as far apart from each other as the campus would allow; it came as no surprise that we didn't say goodbye. Although, at the time I didn't want to hear anything about her, it wasn't long till I started to miss her. I went back to Michigan for the summer and she went back to her hometown Kansas. I still regret never saying goodbye. No matter how hard a goodbye may be, there should always be one. If nothing else just so there is a finality to it all.

I continued to stay drunk most of the time, sometimes even at the video store I was working at. I was still coping with too many things; my grandmother dying, having to give up football, slowly getting better from all the concussions, and for a new twist my father and I had a huge "falling out" and were not speaking to each other anymore. About the end of July I finally hit absolute rock bottom without having to die. I went to a party, got drunk, and passed out; the next morning I woke up next to a naked girl whom I didn't know with drugs lying around.

That was it for me; I knew I had to get clean or I would be dead soon. I also began to realize then that with losing my football scholarship I couldn't afford to go back to school. I hadn't worried about never seeing Kelly again until now. It also occurred to me the sacrifice I had made and would continue to make. I didn't call Kelly to let her know that I wasn't coming back so it was easy to walk away knowing she was mad at me and probably didn't want to see me anymore.

Since I was still getting clean and putting my own young life back together, I would just stay away without contact of any kind. So I stayed completely away knowing that my shattered life could only ruin hers if I was a part of it; at the time that was the greatest gift that I could give to her. Or so I thought.

With her out of my life, it made me see how much she had meant to me; how much I really loved her. She was beautiful, exciting, compassionate, stubborn, and I loved everything about her. She literally made me feel alive and want to be a better person. She could bring out the very best in anyone. The thing that mostly attracted me to her was her faith in God and Humanity. I think it was because I didn't have much and in no small way, she made me want to be a better person.

Kelly was a strong Christian woman even though she didn't put much faith in most churches. She always said that most churches missed the entire point of God. They were too political and the people thought of themselves "holier than thou!" To her God was something simple; believing in God meant complete and utter love for him and the unwavering belief in Christ's resurrection and salvation.

That's all we have to understand about God and Jesus Christ. I didn't really have any belief in a religion and God then, but Kelly opened my eyes to that kind of faith. The other thing that made her even more beautiful than anybody else was her beliefs when it came to sex. She believed very much in sex, but not how most people went about doing it.

Kelly chose a long time ago that she was going to wait and give herself unto someone she truly loved. Lots of people say that they are going to wait, but never stick with that kind of commitment. Kelly however, was not one that gave up so easily, even to the point of being stubborn enough not to give up. What really made her beautiful above all others was the fact that she was a woman that kept her oath as well as being filled with values, morality, and virtue, which is not always easy to find in a woman this day and age. She was the only woman, I would have waited for and how many nineteen year old men could really say that.

With a passionate look like a poet and in a reverent tone, I asked Joe while we were eating pancakes. "Have you ever touched an angel or kissed the soft lips of one while knowing that you were touching the very existence of God? It's to feel just a glimpse of heaven and all its wonder; then to love it more than anything on the face of the earth? Nothing else in the world would matter when standing within her presence; I figured out a long time ago that is the true nature of love. It sounds silly, I know, but it's true."

Joe looked at me with a saddened look. " I felt something like that once before when I first met my girlfriend and I guess I still feel something like that even now when I am around her. You must have loved Kelly very much even then didn't you?"

I answered him back. "You're right, I did love her that much; maybe not enough to marry her when we were only nineteen, but age matters not when it comes to love. The only thing I believe matters about love is realizing it and being honest with whom it is directed towards. No matter how ridiculous it might seem or how embarrassed you might be about it you have nothing to lose by being honest."

At the end of the summer when it was time to go back, I just canceled my financial aid and tuition to the school and left the matter closed. One day when school had already started, I received a call from Kelly wondering why I was not coming back and why I didn't tell her. It was a great surprise to hear from her because I thought she would just forget about me and move on. That would have been the easiest thing to do. It made me feel good when she called me out of concern for it meant that she really did care about me; it also hurt at the same time.

I eventually called her back. Since I was still putting my life back together a lot of things I had wanted to say within a letter I was writing to her, I could say to her now. We talked as if it was the first time we had met; we talked about old times, and tried to say what our hearts had been trying to say for so long.

I knew that she felt the same about me as I did about her, but we were not going to be that vulnerable to each other. I told her that I was sorry for how I'd changed and treated her badly the last few months that we together. We were honest with one another as much as we could possibly be back then. In our sorrow we said goodbye to one another. We knew that it was truly goodbye deep down.

We said we would keep in touch through email or letters and I promised to see her again sometime soon. Maybe we just said the things we wanted to hear, but I think somewhere deep down we both knew that our lives were heading in separate directions and that it was just easier to move on.

I choose to stay home in Michigan for a semester and go to a local community college. Kelly stayed in Kansas and pursued drama and music, which I knew she would succeed at both for she was truly an artist. About that time I had discovered the Romantic writers both in England and America. I began a journey of sucking all the morrow out of life as Thoreau says and began living life to its fullest extent. Life was about to show all its possibilities to each of us, but in different ways.

It did not take long for me to grow restless again back in Michigan so after a few months I left again. This would be the last time I ever lived in Michigan; Colorado would turn out to be home from now on. I transferred into the University of Colorado at Boulder, which was a lot more inexpensive in tuition. Everything I loved about Colorado was nearby; a big city like Denver, great ski resorts like Winter Park, and lots of wilderness for fishing and camping.

Colorado was more than just a new place to live, but a world filled with wonder and a heavenly Revelation. It was a place of inspiration and more possibility than I could ever imagined. I majored in English literature and Communications because it was the only thing at college, I actually liked except for skiing which unfortunately was not listed as a class or part of a degree plan. I really did have a lot of fun there and got to meet some great friends. This is also where I met Steve. We had a lot in common for we were both English majors and loved to ski. We had a lot of our classes together and bartended together at some of the local bars in Boulder. I became a bartender because I figured since I had already spent so much time drinking and spending time in a bar I knew what I was doing and I needed the money so it worked out perfectly.

We also dated a lot of woman in our college years. It wasn't too long before I was putting my ability to play the piano to good use in some of these places we worked at. I wasn't a great piano player or at least I didn't think so, but I had my regular following of fans who craved jazz and blues and classic rock as much as I did. Steve and I were having some good times in college so much so that we became roommates in a small two-bedroom house. I would tell you about some of the wild parties we had there, but to be honest I don't really remember them. To give you some indication about how things were for a while the only furniture we had was inflatable furniture; exactly what two single guys need!

Not too long after I had been back in Colorado I met Carol. She was a Graduate student in the Psychology department. Carol was very beautiful, intelligent, had a great sense of humor, and we had a lot of fun together. I met her as it turned out in a music store and for the next 8 hours we stayed and talked with each other. From that day we didn't spend that much time away from each other.

Carol was from Colorado, from Greeley to be exact. I looked at Joe while he was finishing his fifth cup of coffee and said to him sarcastically. "Carol was a great gal and with her being a Psychologist, I learned a lot about myself in that relationship! She always had a lot of insight. Sometimes it was more than I want to know, but she did make me a better person in a lot of ways. "

Even though, it did not last I still miss her in some ways and hurts to know that I just wasn't that good for her. She was someone that had already lived in the fast lane and just wanted to slow down by having a steady and stable relationship. I on the other hand, I was only twenty and still wanted to be in the fast lane; we had a lot of fun, but it came to an end after only a few months. I realized that in the end she couldn't be with me because I was too self-involved and always-living life to the fullest, sometimes a little too much. Bartending and playing piano in the bars and clubs around the area takes a lot out of you; it is a very stressful life and Carol, being a few years older than I just couldn't live that life anymore.

She always said that there was a lot to be said for a peaceful and quiet evening at home; although I did not necessarily understand that then believe me I do now! She was really wonderful and a great lover, but sometime in the summer we parted ways. I was still restless, so I headed out to New Orleans a town that was always filled with excitement. I only meant to stay for a week, but I stayed two months and tried to make it as a piano player. It didn't quite happen like I planned and I was home in Colorado just before school started for the fall semester.

The great thing about the experience was the excitement of feeling alive at every turn. To me, it was about not caring about success or failure, but the experience itself. In those two months living in New Orleans I grew up fast and saw so many shades of life. It didn't stop me from being reckless, but the way I saw the world was forever changed and New Orleans is definitely the place to do that.

When I got back to Boulder, I continued to do the same things I always did; I played piano anywhere I could. I paid my way with bartending gigs and I slowly finished my degree. About the time I got back, Steve and I had figured out that we just couldn't live together anymore and if we were going to remain friends then we just have to live in separate homes. Steve sarcastically said. "Yeah, Blake was a real pain in the ass and anal to; he just couldn't stand anything being dirty."

I laughed. "Well, at least I wasn't a complete slob and besides, I never got any sleep with you banging on the walls all night long with whatever girl you decided to bring home that night." So I moved out and found a place of my own in a small one bedroom apartment."

That semester, I also discovered the radio. I found that with my personality and sarcastic sense of humor, I wasn't too bad on the air. I started doing a communications degree, then while doing weekly segments of the college radio station. I did everything from the sports to political commentary. The radio turned out to be, as a minister would say, my calling in life.

I could be anybody I wanted on the radio and say anything or at least almost anything. The FCC is funny like that. Some people find acting so they can be other people or the play the character that are far from their own. Radio was that for me. Somebody else passed through my life at that time. She would end up being a blessing in disguise. Her name was Lori and I knew her from some of my English classes. We always seemed to have the same classes together and in the fall semester it turned out she needed a roommate. Lori was a preacher's daughter, but was far from being good. If you want a trip on the wild side , she was the girl for you. I loved every minute of it,

It wasn't that she was a terrible human being or some kind of whore; she was just very rebellious and lived life to the extreme. She was the type of person that challenged life at every turn and it made her very exciting. For guys like me, it's too easy to fall for a girl that. I wasn't strong enough to resist. Lori was working in a jewelry store and couldn't afford to live by herself so she moved in with me and became my roommate. Even though there were two bedrooms, most of the time we just shared a bed.

There were times when we were very serious with each other and then times we just lived together and dated other people. Lori knew me very well and I knew her well; she knew me almost as well as somebody else once did. We had a lot of fun together and it made it great because she was very much an outdoors type of girl so we went camping and skiing a lot. We also partied a great deal together and it took its toll on both of us. Even though, I did not drink as much as I did when I was depressed for that period of my life, I unfortunately drank way too much when I partied with her. She was a redheaded Irish gal and could out-drink any man. Just one more thing that made me attracted to her.

Lori was also very impulsive and most of the time did things at a moment's notice. One time during spring break, she had the urge to travel to New York City so we did for a couple of days. Both of us had never been so we pulled together what money we had, found the cheapest airfare, and stayed in the cheapest hotel we could find. We did the tourist thing, while seeing the sites and it turned out to be a wild and crazy adventure that both of us would never forget.

Lori was fun to be with, but I knew that she and I lasting forever would never be. There was always something inside of me keeping me from falling in love with her, and she knew it as plain as the sun rises in the east and sets in the west. Even though she knew this, Lori never made it an issue and stayed with me anyway.

Sometimes, while seeing each other, she would have to live on her own or with someone else. I believe that it was that kind of restlessness between us that allowed us to be with each other as long as we did, or at least remain friends. Anyway, she blessed me in a way because through no fault of her own, she made me realize that I was in love with someone else and always had been. I had never admitted it out loud before and now while dating Lori the truth became clear. Through all of this Lori and I were with each other for the better part of two years.

Almost three years had gone since I last saw Kelly and I started to wonder about her. I found an old picture of her that I had from when we were dating. Something inside of me had to find out what had happened to her. I called a friend of mine from the radio station named Ben, who was a computer genius.

He was just the right person to help me find her for he was known as the CU-FBI database on the account that he could find anybody for you in the world (for a price of course). Ben was a computer hacker of sorts and had resources over the Internet that could find anybody, so I employed him to find Kelly for me. It only took a six pack of beer.

My friend Ben was able to find an e-mail address and a phone number for Kelly in the Wichita, Kansas area. I waited around for a few days with the information before using it. To be quite honest, I was scared as hell; I didn't know what she would say or even if she wanted to hear from me at all.

Ben and Steve were not helping either! They would be "kidding around" with me by calling me a "wussie" or I could say to her when I called her that calling her was part of the 12-step program I was on. Well. After enough prodding by my friends, I finally emailed her and believe it or not she replied back.

She wasn't mad at me at all and was really glad to hear from me. That night I called her and it was like old times and the memories I had about being with her came flashing back like it was yesterday.

Apparently Kelly was going to a school in Wichita for a year doing a drama workshop. We caught-up with each other and told what had happened with our lives for the last three years. We laughed out loud and comforted each other over our losses, but most important, we repaired all the hurt between us. We must have talked for hours and finally we got to the one part of the conversation that I was dreading, our love lives.

Kelly calmly asked me in a quiet but solemn tone, if I was dating anybody hoping that I would not answer, but I did. I didn't know exactly what to say so I told her "no" even though I was still seeing Lori. At the time it seemed like that if I had told her the truth, then our reunion would have ended right then and there. A tragedy for sure and I knew that I couldn't bear it. I told her that I had, had a few relationships over the years, but nothing ever seemed to last. She just simply said to me. "Well, that's good," and didn't say anything else for what seemed like an eternity

Kelly could not say anything else, no smart-ass remarks, no reassuring comments, and no compassionate clichés as if to tell me that she was glad I wasn't some deep depressed individual, but on the other hand that I was not in any committed relationship heading for marriage. I asked her if she was dating anybody and she was totally honest with me; she had been seeing someone for about a year and was madly in love with him.

Hearing that broke my heart, but I couldn't be too surprised, after all we had not seen each other in almost three years. Kelly told me that they would probably graduate at the same time and she knew that he was the one she wanted to spend the rest of her life with. She also told me that she and this other guy had talked about marriage and planned to be married not too long after graduation. I could feel the cosmic sticking and twisting in my heart. It was painful to hear her joy on the other end of the phone when talking about this guy,

My first instinct was to tell not to do it because I was in love with her even though I didn't want to be married. Not exactly fair. I didn't say anything like that and just wished her the best of luck. Kelly used tell me the man she would marry would be awesome and a true gift of God. My only hope was that this guy was awesome or at least for his sake he had better be!

Kelly and I parted that night as the closest of friends and I promised myself that I would keep in-touch with her from now on, but again, when you're young, promises fade away quickly. They become empty words until we are old enough to understand the

5

Even though Lori and I were not exactly serious with each other at the time, I didn't want her to find out what I had done. It wasn't that I thought Lori wouldn't understand. It's not like I even cheated on her. I was too afraid of having to admit to her and everybody else out loud that I was still in love with Kelly. Lori found out anyway and got angry with me for not being honest with her. To this day, I still don't know how she found out about the phone call. Maybe it was God's way of telling me to hide anything from a woman you're involved with. Honesty was definitely the best policy no matter how much it hurt.

She left me and moved out for a while. Unfortunately, our relationship would never be the same because of this. Eventually, Lori moved back and became my roommate again months later, but nothing was ever the same and we went on being gracious to one another. While Lori was away, though, I kept part of my promise and called Kelly a couple times. It made me feel good to have her back in my life again, even if we were just phone friends. Just hearing her voice made my life better.

We acted like long lost friends, which I guess we were in a way. We were able to tell each other our deepest and most personal thoughts, be objective with one another, and comfort each other when it was needed. But it would only be short-lived.

There were a couple of times Kelly actually called me up crying her heart out over something because she felt there wasn't anybody else she could talk to. This just made me even crazier for her and question every day why I didn't get in my car, drive to where she was, and tell her how much in love with her I was. It wasn't necessarily enough to marry her, but to try and be the one constant in her life as she could be for me. I put myself in the friend zone as harsh as that way just to be a part of her life. Might seem pathetic, but I was a part of her life and that's what mattered.

One Particular night, I called her to see how she was doing and if school for her had become a little less stressful. We talked about what was going on with us since last we spoke and then all of a sudden she told me the most dreadful news; well it was for me anyway. Kelly told me that her boyfriend had definitely proposed marriage to her, but wanted to wait till they both graduated. She still yes, though.

Even though they were not getting married right away, they pretty much promised themselves to each other. This was not exactly the news I needed to hear at this point and time! I didn't know what to say to her so the only words I had the courage to speak were. "Well, that's good." I really didn't say anything else to her and as if perfect timing my doorbell rang. Steve and Ben had come by to see if I wanted to get a few drinks.

Seizing the perfect opportunity to end the conversation, I told her that some friends had come by and I would call her back later in the week. That was the last time I spoke to Kelly. It would be years later before I ever talked to her or even saw her again. I can't honestly say why I didn't call Kelly back; maybe I felt that she was already out of my reach or maybe I was too scared to go after her.

All I did was hide behind the mask of my own shame and guilt telling everybody that I was over her. The truth was ,she still consumed my heart and the pain from not being with her was buried deep down, but I tried forgetting Kelly and moving on with my life. When one truly loves someone that love is never forgotten just misplaced sometimes.

It also came to pass that many things would unravel in my life. After a while Lori would leave my life forever. She graduated the next semester and moved away. She took a teaching position in another country, Argentina I think, teaching English and

Literature at an American school there. Lori and I had a lot of fun over the years while we were together, but we were not right for each other and eventually parted somewhat as friends.

We promised to stay in touch with each other and I did receive a couple of postcards from her, but that was it. We never really saw each other again and eventually lost touch with each other completely. The worst part, it didn't even bother me. The last thing I heard about her was she had gotten married to someone from another country about three years ago.

When I think of her I am reminded that some people only pass through your life for a season, they show you what's possible, they restore the balance in your life and then they are gone, never to be heard from again. Hopefully this is what Lori and I did for each other , at least she did it for me. Although when we were together in whatever way we admitted that either of us had never been happier here. This kind of feeling can bring comfort lost souls in love.

Other bad things happened to me in the next year like spending a few nights in Jail for not paying my speeding tickets or putting myself so much in debt that I was evicted from my house. Even though things like this happened my joy in romanticism was restored as well as my faith in life. I became very much a romantic again and enjoyed all there was to enjoy about life even though the darkness that seemed to still remain.

I had remembered something that I heard a long time ago and perhaps it's true Beauty; romance, passion, and even love are the things that we are very much alive for. It also made me realize in the face of disaster that life is still full of many and wonderful surprises.

Within the next year I completed my English and Communication degree along with Steve. I didn't know what kind of job I was going to get although I could have been a professional Bartender, but it was not what I wanted to do for a career. It was fun, but still too much of a job, Steve took a job at a Denver radio station in the administration helping in advertising and the human resources department. Well, as it turned out they were looking for nighttime DJs for their all night classic rock hour.

Steve gave them a few of my broadcasts from the College Station and they offered me a job after only three minutes of listening to those tapes. Yes, it was pretty bizarre because one day I was just sitting at home looking through the want-ads and I got this phone call from the station manager telling me that I had been hired and he was hoping I wouldn't take another job. It took all about 3 seconds to say "yes" to the job. This is how I got a job at the radio station mainly thanks to Steve.

Steve softly spoke up and said. "Yeah, that's what I am here for, I'm always saving his butt in some aspect; you wouldn't believe how many favors he owes me." We all just laughed while sitting in the diner at three in the morning.

Steve and I both moved into the city of Denver living at different places of course and began our careers in the radio business. When I first started out I had to work nights and wasn't all that great, but I got to be a DJ to a classic rock station. Although the company that the station was owned by had other stations like techno and easy listening (that were all horrible) within the building the classic rock station always had the most fun.

We also tended to be the craziest station, which was just fine by me. After about a year of being there I didn't have to work nights anymore and I got more popular around the Denver area. Also, about that time the radio station was trying something new; we were becoming a little more involved in politics. We would have open forums on some of the local and national issues.

We would also invite local and national politicians to the station to get their message across, and most importantly we would get to make fun of everybody. After a while we were turning into another *Saturday Night Live* and people loved it.

The ratings were just getting higher the more involved we got in the political scene. It's funny how a political format can do that at a radio station...a subject never ceases to divide people. I personally became really popular with my hour-long segment twice a week where I got to interview a political figure and got to be satirical with him or her. It was like my own *Rush Limbaugh Show* just a little more discreet and I actually presented solutions to the person I was interviewing while still being funny. My career couldn't be going better and I was having a fun time with my job. That was important...I never wanted to be my old man and work a job I hated just for a paycheck.

Remember , I told you before, with all good things there are tragedies that can come with it. Since I had become somewhat famous in the Denver area I did not have any shortage of women I could date. My life still remained in the fast lane when it came to this one area. Even though I did not party and stay out as much as I did during my college years, my love life didn't slow down and it wore me out at times. Steve used to always "kid me around" that a steady relationship didn't mean steady sex. I knew he was right, but that didn't stop me from being promiscuous. But, hey, a promiscuous person is just someone who's getting more sex than you are

I liked the fact I didn't have to be serious with someone, to still have somewhat of a love life. Although, there were still consequences to my actions and I think God would remind me of that so I could be humble from time to time.

Over the past few years, before I was married there were a few instances where some of the women I had been sleeping with thought they were pregnant with my child. That would always scare me because I knew then that I couldn't raise a child and would be a terrible father. Also, it might have been some of the women I was sleeping with that made me fear having children as well.   To tell you the truth, it also usually meant my fears proved just how guilty I was feeling with my life style. It always seemed fun, but really, it's just more exhausting and not always in a good way.

I told Joe. "Please do not misunderstand me in that I condone that kind of lifestyle or that I judge anybody who lives that kind of lifestyle, each to their own. It's been my experience that people usually engage in that kind of lifestyle to fill a void within their life. For most people its loneliness, but for me it was a pain buried deep down within the heart; I'm not making excuses just giving you a few reasons why."

This is the way my life went for the next couple of years. I never had any serious relationships; most of them were just short-lived. I became more famous through the radio station as well as my political shows that were on the air (I had about three different shows involving political issues and satire now) and for the most part I was generally happy with my career.

I was getting to do what I really loved which is more than most people can say about their jobs, but it still wasn't enough. I found out that one could have lots of money, lots of friends, and have a great career doing something they really love, but still be miserable. Somehow, I had known this, but I never really believed it to be true until it happened to me. So like most people in these situations I was getting depressed and starting to drink too much again because there was nothing in my life that really meant anything to me. I was simply going through the motions.

It had been a great few years with me and my career; I was also maturing in life. I had almost everything anybody needed to be happy in life except the most important thing, love. After watching a movie called Don Juan De Marco something very important on how to live life started to make sense to me. Believe or not I was able to learn something from the movie that was very much true about love and life. It made perfect sense In the spirit of Lord Byron and Don Juan, I learned that there are only four questions of value in life and they all have one commonality. The questions are these; what is sacred, what is the spirit made of, what is worth living for, and what is worth dying for? The answer to all of them is love; the most important thing to contentment and perfect happiness. The writer of that movie really nailed it.

Now, love comes in all sizes and forms, and there are many different levels of love. As long as you love someone more than yourself then all can be good. With

Love, no matter how bad anything seems, everything can still be right and not be quite as bad as you might have thought. I believe this as much I believe in God himself.

I remembered what John Lennon once wrote, "All you need is love." Sure, it's a little hokey, but it doesn't make it less true. Despite my Romanticism and border-lined depression, the sun would make the flower known as love inside of me bloom once again.

It had been about four years now since I last spoke to Kelly and even longer since I last saw her. Summer had started as well as the baseball season; that always brought excitement to the Denver area because of the Colorado Rockies. Well, one day the station was out of the ball park doing a broadcast.

I was doing one of my shows out there trying to get our listeners hyped up for the baseball season and getting a chance to make fun of all the high priced baseball players. At the station we all loved baseball, but couldn't stand the outrageous salaries some of these guys were being paid especially when some of them would whine about the fact they were only making ten million dollars a season.

Anyway, we were interviewing kids out at the ballpark about what they thought of the outrageous salaries and the salary cap in baseball. This is when I got the biggest surprise of my life. One of the programmers for the show would go and find kids in the stands to bring up to our booth to be interviewed. A couple of the kids she found were with a big group from a citywide youth center that specialized in teaching inner-city kids the arts.

Anyway, they were all here for the baseball game and the youth worker that accompanied the kids to the booth to make sure we didn't exploit them turned out to be Kelly. Yeah. I was shocked.

6

I saw her while I was still on the air as she was walking the kids to the booth and I seemed to lose all of my words. Not a good thing to do on the radio. Of all the dumb luck, it was Kelly who came to my booth that day. I can't really say if it was fate or the planets were misaligned or maybe some other cosmic phenomenon that causes lovers to cross paths, but my life was forever changed after that day.

I was so tongue tied after seeing her that my Co-host had to finish that part of the show. Kelly saw me too, and looked at me with shocking amazement; last ten steps to the booth were the longest moments in time for the both if us. I quickly put down my headset and ran over to her; there was no walking involved it was pure running. It was like a dream, but a dream that no one would ever want to wake up from.

It was a place where there is no sorrow or pain, a place of only joy and peace, a place that could only be known as the enduring myth of heaven. That place was the distance between us. Everybody around us thought I had totally lost my mind, the kids hid behind her when I came up to her thinking that I was going to harm them or something of that nature.

I still didn't know what to say to her, but we both just looked at each other what seemed for the longest time and then she finally said. " Hi Blake, how are you; you don't have to be so shocked… it's me."

I finally spoke in a quiet tone. "I'm sorry, this is a big surprise, I just can't believe it's really you." There were so many things that we both wanted to say, but through the total shock of seeing each other, nothing seemed to come out. Strange, yes, but it does happen. There was only a look of regret, a look of love, and both of us being in complete awe of each other. Time went by so fast, that when I looked back at my Co-host he was shouting back at me that we were on the air in 30 seconds.

I looked at Kelly and said. "Please don't go, I want to talk to you after the show so promise me you are not going to disappear." Kelly just casually laughed at me and replied. "No, I won't run out quite yet, besides, I can't leave without the kids."

I smiled. "Oh yeah, that's right.

We quickly finished our interviews and the show. I didn't really care if we were funny or not or how successful the show went. The only thing that was important to me was that Kelly was back in my life again, no matter how short our time would be together. I for one was not going to let her disappear.

When our work at the ballpark was complete, I asked Kelly if she was doing anything that night and if she would join me for dinner. She didn't hesitate to accept and I took her to dinner a few hours later. The one thing that utterly amazed me about her was the fact she was still as beautiful as the first day we met. I personally had changed quite a bit. I was starting to lose my hair and I wasn't even thirty years old yet. Never considered myself handsome, but Kelly was absolutely stunning. Kelly and I told each other what had happened in our lives over the past few years and talked a little bit of old times.

Kelly had graduated from the college she was attending in Wichita, Kansas about three years ago with a theater and education degree. She took a job with an organization that specialized in setting up youth centers in inner cities and teaching the kids the arts. Kelly got to travel around to different places helping children enjoy some of the things she loved like music, dance, and theater.

The one thing I was really surprised about was the fact she was not married and

I was really, really glad of that. We were at a little Italian place that I was a regular at because for one she loved Italian food and the food there tasted like sweet honey on a spring day compared to any other Italian restaurant that I knew of. I needed all the brownie points I could get. And I knew the Androlini family that owned the place would take care of us just fine through their wide selection of wine and "fantastic" pasta!

It didn't take me long during our dinner to ask her why she was not married. She started to explain in a calm but regretful tone. "Robert and I were happy for a long time and I did love him. I wanted to spend the rest of my life with him or so I thought. Everything between us up to graduation was good and then once we graduated and started our careers things changed between us. It changed like overnight. It was weird!"

She looked at me intently and continued. "Robert was an Architect and got a job with a large firm in Kansas City, but first he got to do a program overseas through the company. He was going to Italy for the summer and he wanted me to go with him; his parents were willing to pay for it as a pre-wedding gift. By the time we graduated we were already engaged, but I have to admit that once that happened, it was never the same between us. Robert was very much concerned with his career and where it was going. He wanted to get married and have a family, but it came a very distant second to his career."

She shook her in disbelief and said. "Even though I did not want to have children right away I was ready to start a family and part of the reason I did was to fill a void within me that had been there for a long time. I still don't know what that void was, but now I see it wasn't being the typical family person I had wanted to have so much and I thought that was going to fill it. I found out something else. It wasn't having a family with Robert and being married to him that was going to fill it either and believe it or not Robert knew that before I did. He wanted me to follow him anywhere his career took him, but I just couldn't do that and forsake what I wanted to do in life" Kelly said as she continued with her story.

Kelley came to the end of her story and a very honest realization and finished by saying. "Well to make a long story short, we called off the engagement right before he left and parted ways. I have to hand it to him before he left, he said to me like a gentleman that he hoped someday I would find whatever I needed to fill that void even if was not him. Robert was a good man and I loved him in a way, but I can see now that I didn't love him enough and the roads in life we were taking, were very different so it would have never worked between us."

I couldn't help but be curious about the void in her life so I asked her about it. She just simply replied back. "Not tonight. I will tell you when we are both ready. " And then she just smiled that beautiful, gorgeous smile that seems to go on for days. It was a smile that you couldn't help but get lost in. I didn't press the issue. All the issues between us would eventually come out. The day was coming sooner than we realized, when we would eventually have to be totally honest with the other. It scared the hell out of me.

Kelly wanted to know about my life and how it had turned out so I told her a little bit. I didn't go into great detail about living my life in the fast lane and my romantic escapades. I didn't want her to see me as some kind of lowlife she had to quickly get away from. Anything to get Kelly to stick around just a little bit longer

She asked me about the radio station that I worked at and about what we did in my shows. She told me that from what she had heard at the ballpark, my Co-host and I were pretty funny and liked to have a good time on the radio. It was true, we did, I have had some outrageous shows over the years. Kelly asked me what the zaniest thing I had ever done on the radio was. I told her about the Colorado Congressmen interview about a year before that where we had a live studio audience that was going to ask him questions instead of calling in.

In a humorous tone I told her the story "We had a Congressman who got photographed by a tabloid coming out of a hotel with two of the Bronco cheerleaders. The funny thing about it all was he was an ultra-conservative and tried to display himself as a moral Christian who prided himself on family values. Getting caught having an affair didn't help his image. "

The story made me laugh, but I continued with it, "Well, there was no way he could deny what happened and make everybody believe that he hadn't had an affair with the two cheerleaders, what can I say, perception can be a bitch. The Congressmen were scheduled to be interviewed on my show the next week, so Steve, who is my best friend and one of my bosses, and I decided that we were going to surprise the Congressmen. On the day of the interview Steve and I switched the live audience with the entire wait-staff from the Hooter's restaurant down the street and completely surprised the congressmen." I continued.

Everybody at the station thought it was funny except the owners and the congressmen, but our ratings for that particular show went through the roof. The Hooter's girls asked him important questions ranging from abortion to same-sex marriages; apparently there were a few lesbian couples among the group. We personally had a great time with the Congressmen, but he couldn't answer the questions like he wanted with all the distractions he had because the Hooter's staff in their skimpy outfits were distracting him. Needless to say, he's never been a return guest at the station and probably will never be; Steve and I also got in trouble for what we pulled with the station owners, but our audiences absolutely loved the show so we weren't fired."

Kelly gave me a sarcastic smile and replied. "You guys are cruel, but that does not surprise me about you." Kelly knew me all too well because I have always been a guy who would do anything for a good laugh. Kelly was also one who could appreciate the humor in a stunt like that and this is one reason we did get along sometimes; it always helps to have a similar sense of humor with a woman. Laughter can definitely get you through the bad times.

We stayed at the restaurant for hours until it was time for them to close just talking and when it was time, I walked her back to her place like a perfect gentleman not expecting anything else for the evening. For me, an evening like this had not happened for a long time. I told her that I wanted to see her again and keep seeing her as long as she was in Denver since she tended to travel often through her job. She said that she would like that and had enjoyed the evening very much. It was the best news that I had heard in a long time. As I was about to turn away and go home, I felt that there was one last thing I should say to her.

I turned around. "Kelly, I'm sorry for not ever calling you back like I said I would or for never coming back to see you. I know that I have been a real jerk and it had nothing to do with you. I was just afraid that you would tell me that you never wanted to see me again and to be honest, I don't know if I could have lived with that and even now I still feel that way."

I did the one thing I should have done a long time ago; I was humble enough to really apologize to her for any hurt that I may have caused. Sometimes it takes a lot of growing up before something like that can be done. Kelly just walked up to me

and kissed me and time seemed to stop.
When we were done, she looked at me and
smiled. "Blake, call me tomorrow." That one
line was the all the forgiveness I needed.

7

I knew that Kelly was not going to be in Denver very long since she was only helping to get the local youth center she was at up and running, but it didn't stop us from spending a lot of time together. We talked to each other every day and night, sometimes falling asleep to the sound of each other's voice on the phone. All our free time, it seemed, was spent with each other. It felt just like the when we were in college again. They say you can never get those great moments in your life again, but damn, was this pretty close.

Kelly and I acted like young lovers again always being romantic with each other, telling our most personal secrets to each other, and kissing whenever we could. That is the one thing I always like the best with Kelly, just getting to kiss her. Every kiss was special. She was a great kisser too, passionate and sensual, and every kiss felt like It could last for days. I know time didn't really stop when we kissed, but felt that way. The rest of my love life disappeared and I only saw one woman for a change. The right woman, I kept telling myself.

Even though I did not see much of my friends anymore, they all liked being around me more because of how happy I had become now that Kelly was in my life again. It was true, I was very happy because like a true gift of God, I was with Kelly again. That was the only way to explain it,

One particular night we were at my place cooking dinner. We had just decided to have a nice quiet evening with a delicious home cooked dinner, a bottle of wine, and a movie. Kelly had, had a very long and stressful day and was very much in need of a relaxing evening. She had not changed all that much in the fact she always worked too hard and her life was filled with too many activities.

We tried to watch the movie, but it wasn't too long before we started to talk. Our conversation started to get serious and I mean really serious. Steve had been prodding me for a week now to tell Kelly the truth about how I really felt about her. He had known about my love for her even before I admitted it out loud; he also was there for me through all the hurtful relationships I had, had in the past. Steve was my best friend and very much like a brother to me so he knew everything about me and Kelly as well as how I had been in love with her ever since I first saw her.

Honestly, I was afraid of what she might think if I told her the truth and worst of all, she wouldn't feel the same; even then I don't know if I could take that. The truth is most human beings have a hard time being honest about their true feelings in the fear that the other person will not feel the same. Sometimes it is too hard to live with and we never know how to cope with life after that. Sometimes the hardest thing is letting a loved one go, to set something free and hope it comes back. Half the time is just letting go.

As our conversation got more serious and I knew that I had to tell her so I did. The words were not exactly poetic and sometimes I fumbled them, but after a long pause I finally said to her. "Okay, time to finally be honest and admit what I've known for a long time then here it is. Kelly I fell in love with you when I first saw you as silly as that might sound, but ever since then I have been in love with you and it has only grown stronger. I cannot remember a time feeling more alive and content than when I was with you and this is the one pain that I have had buried deep down inside of me for so long. Because of it, I have ruined my fair share of relationships and never been able to make it go away. Even though I have always felt this way, I want you to know that I love you enough to let you go and walk away if you want me to. You need to know the truth and if we both have to move on in our lives, I wanted to do it with a clear conscious."

Kelly sat in front of me with a surprised look on her face. Time seemed to stand still as she sat there not saying anything. It was awkward. I wanted to say something else, but I've been known to talk the moment away so I just waited for her to say something. Finally, she spoke in a joyous tone. "You're right, we must move on with a clear conscious and I think you should know the truth about me. Blake I was in love with you then even though we might have just been two foolish teenagers. You opened up my life and made it worth something even though I couldn't stand to be around you those last few months we were together; I think I finally understand now what happened to you. Unfortunately the tragedies within our lives can affect our feelings...affect what we do and what we say. It took me a long time to realize that it wasn't your fault. it was just something that happened. I also spent a long trying forgive you for walking away like you did and never keeping in touch with me, but I didn't try to stay in touch with you either. It took a long time to move on and Robert helped me to do that in many ways; maybe that's why it was so easy to love him. You see I realized that it wasn't enough with him because I still loved you deep down. It was easier to just move on.

We both just sat there looking at each other, hoping the other one would say it; to say the thing that would keep us from walking out of each other's lives. Unfortunately, we were both too stubborn to say it. What it did was create a bigger bridge between us.

I finally spoke up and told her. "Well, I think this is fantastic and yes, maybe this was little too much like soap opera dialogue, but I am glad we could be honest. I know you will be leaving soon and if nothing else, maybe we should just say that we were each other's first loves and leave it at that."

Kelly was shocked. "Really, that's it."

I was taken back by her comment. "What do you mean?"

"You can't just say it, can you?"

"I just said, I love you, what else should I say?"

Kelly shook her head, not wanting to believe what she just heard. "We are not going to at least talk about marriage."

"I didn't think we were ready to talk about marriage."

"That's usually something you talk about after professing your love to someone...especially your first love."

"Look, I hadn't even thought about it. I was just glad to have you back in my life."

Kelly started to get angry. "You're still scared. It's just like the time we talked about it our first year of college."

"You know how I feel about marriage...I don't necessarily think we have to be married to be together."

She didn't like hearing that. Kelly was still very traditional in a lot of ways. The next step after dating, if you really love someone was marriage. Anything short of that was someone who didn't really want to commit. It was insult to suggest otherwise, especially when love was involved. I knew she was angry with me. When I tried to say something else, she cut me off. "I understand why you think that and even thought you're full of it...the worst part is you haven't even asked me to stay."

I was shocked. It didn't even occur to me to ask her to stay. And to be honest, I thought it was a foregone conclusion that she would stay after professing our love to one another. However, there is no such thing when it comes to women. She left early that night to get some rest for her busy day tomorrow We agreed to meet each other for lunch the next day and try to put this behind us, but things like that just don't fade away.

The next day when I saw her during my lunch hour we had a picnic lunch within a nearby park. The radiant sun seemed to shine extra bright in the morning, but clouds were quickly rolling in; a sign that the day was not going to be as good as previously thought. We sat on the park bench just eating our hot dogs and talking, but we didn't talk about us. We talked about everything else, so we didn't have to. It was an awkward. We didn't want to ruin anything between us to we avoided the real conversation as much as much possible.

Finally, Kelly spoke up. " Blake, I am leaving tomorrow night for another city and youth center; I'm leaving a week early to get settled because it looks like I am going to be there for a while."

It made me angry to listen to her it. I tried to search for the right words so I just kept it simple. "Where are going now... I mean too far away in case I want to visit"

Kelly, in a soft voice, replied. "I am going to San Diego; it was either that or Atlanta so I chose the beach and warm weather all year long."

Neither of us said anything for a few moments, although it seemed like an eternity.

Then, with a desperate plea and all the courage I could muster, I said to her. "Look, I don't want you to go; we only just walked back into our lives again."

Kelly just simply asked. Why don't you want me to go and I know you love me, but it's not enough."

"Do you want me to propose, right here and now?"

"No, because it wouldn't really be your choice... you would just be doing to make me stay."

"If I ask you to marry, then I do it because I choose to."

She gently smiled. "I know you think that, but you wouldn't be proposing because you really wanted to. It would be something out of convenience...just to get me to stay."

I was dumbfounded. I didn't understand what she was getting at. "What do you want me to say...if I were to ask you to marry me, isn't that a good thing?"

"Most of the time, but if you did...I would want you to do it because you really wanted to." Kelly didn't say anything else after that. She gathered her things and returned to work. There wasn't anything else to say.

All of my life, I had been afraid of marriage. Afraid that it would never work out no matter how much I might love someone. And I was even more afraid that she would never love me enough. They say love is enough, but I'm not sure that's true. At this point, I didn't know what to do anymore or if I did, I couldn't admit it out loud.

8

I eventually ended up at Steve's place and recounted the day's events to him. I even went as far to tell him what she had said to me and that I didn't understand. He just offered the best advice he could. "Blake I have known you for a lot of years and seen the many relationships you have been through over the years, but I can't tell what to do in this situation. This is something you have to figure out and the sad thing is you know what to do, but you're too stubborn to do it. Do you know where you're lucky and how many people would love to be in your shoes; you know who you love with all your heart and you have the perfect chance to keep that person from walking out your life forever. An opportunity like that doesn't come often and your happiness only depends on what you do with it."

I eventually went home and ended up in bed after a few glasses of whisky. Drowning the pain seemed like the best option. The next day, I arrived at work late and wasn't very happy. I had almost forgotten that I had to interview Richard Langley the Republican Senator from Colorado.

He was a regular on my show every few months trying to have good public relations with the state of Colorado. He always chose our station because he was friends with one of the station owners and we were the best station for him to prove he was a likable guy with a great sense of humor. This was something every politician needed if he or she was going to have a good persona with the public. I did the interview quicker than usual and the show wasn't as humorous as it usually had been in the past.

When it was done, I just returned to the lounge to have a coke and a smile so to speak, or at least try. Steve walked in and wanted to know how I was this morning, but his friendly comforts didn't work at all. Just as Steve was about to walk out the

Senator popped his head in to say goodbye and see if everybody was okay. The senator, even though he was a politician and had to be friendly to everyone was actually pretty good friends with a lot of us at the radio station. He could be very personable when he wasn't running for office.

He said. "If you don't mind me asking what's wrong; I know something's bothering you because your interview wasn't as funny as usual."

Before I could even respond, Steve spoke up in a sarcastic tone. "Oh, don't mind him Senator, the woman he's in love with and has been for a long, long time is leaving today. And he won't go after her and tell her that he wants to spend the rest of his life with her."

The Senator just laughed and asked me. "Is this true Blake?"

I replied. "So what if it is, I don't need everybody's opinion on how I'm screwing up and being an idiot."

The Senator just looked at me like a teacher and said. "Just remember you're the one who said it and I can see you have it already figured out, but taking a wild guess... the subject of marriage came up and you don't want to be married."

"It's more complicated than that. I was going to propose, yesterday and she pretty much admitted that she wouldn't have said yes."

The Senator with a sarcastic look, simply said "You don't get it; to her it's wanting to marry her that matters...not willing to. There's a difference. No matter what your fears are, it's that you want to be committed to her and you want to spend the rest of your life with her, that's what she's looking for."

The senator admitted out loud what I already knew, but was still afraid to say. The thing is I loved Kelly that much and wanted to spend forever with her. It should have been that easy. Just a few simple words, that's all it would take.

The Senator continued being the teacher and with a hearty laugh said, "Well, I guess it's time to be a man of the people and give some words of inspiration. Blake, Steve let me tell you what I have learned over the years about women. Believe it or not, I was married once and through my ex-wife, I learned that what women want most out of men is for us to be willing to get married, even though we are afraid of marriage and to make a fool out-of-ourselves for them especially in front of lots of people."

I gave him a strange look, but the Senator continued. "If we can do that, it shows how much we really love them and how committed to them we really are. You see, when I first met my ex-wife Caroline we were really romantic with each other; we would write each other little love notes, I'd bring home flowers and surprise her, and we would have the occasional romantic breakfast in bed. Our life was pretty simple because it was before I ever ran for public office, but as soon as my first campaign happened for the 'house' things changed between us. She couldn't handle being a politician's wife because I was never home and I put my marriage and family second to my career. After an affair and being in the public eye my marriage with Caroline ended; after seven years of marriage, Caroline had enough and left me."

The senator changed his tone. It was more somber, now "Unfortunately, I did not do anything to prevent her from divorcing me because I always thought she would realize how much she really loved me and come back, but the truth is I was the one at fault for our marriage ending. She had every right to leave me for the way I had acted and it was the best thing for her. I didn't realize this until it was too late, until I lost her, and now the only thing I live with is regret. I have had a lot of romantic escapades with many beautiful women, but none of them can replace Caroline and the love I had for her, Blake, I would trade every affair, romantic interlude, all the money I've made, and my career as a politician for one more chance with her because she was the one thing of value in my life. If you want my advice then go after Kelly. Do it if you still have a chance and it sounds like to me you do"

I was still confused and distraught. I was hurt, but most of all, I was tired of feeling that way. Steve had an intense look and responded. "Blake, he's right and you know he's right. And if you don't get off your ass and go get her then I won't be your friend anymore because I won't listen to your complaints about how she got away."

I looked at Steve and said. "That's a little harsh, don't you think, you'll quit being my friend if I make a mistake again."

Steve gave me a strange look. "I mean it Blake, don't screw this up, I don't know if I can be your friend anymore if you do." I gave him a dirty look as he laughed at his comment.

I stood up and faced the two other men in the room like a man on trial before the judge gave out the sentence. "I know you guys are right; I think I've always known what to do, but...

Steve replied. "You've been too much of a chicken shit."

I was surprised by the comment. "What!"

"You heard me, you're a chicken shit. But as men, we're bound to be one at some point in our lives."

He was right and I didn't need to admit because he already knew he was right. I simply said. "Okay...Kelly, may not want to see me ever again, but I have to

take that chance. Steve. I am not going to
be back for the rest of the day."

Steve just smiled. "Well, it's about
time you pull your head out of your head,
and don't worry, I already clocked you out
for the rest of the day."

I replied back with a shocked look.
"Steve you're a good friend, but I don't
know how I am going to do this because she
lives across town and I'll never make there
in time with evening traffic."

The senator just laughed at us and
said. "Well, I guess that's what I'm her here
for today; we'll just take my helicopter and
get there in no time."

I just looked at the Senator with a
dumbfounded look. "You have a helicopter;
whatever happened to limos?"

He sarcastically replied back. "Limos
are for Congressmen, a senator always
travels in style, that's why we have
helicopters. Now, come on Blake, we can't
let any more time slip away and I'll take
care of the large crowd; they'll be waiting for
us when we arrive."

I was confused. "Crowd, what are
talking about; what does that have to do

with me getting the girl. All I was going to do was knock on her door like a normal person and I don't think I need any help with that."

The senator shook his head and replied. "If I've learned anything in my profession, a huge crowd there it will make it harder for her to say "no" and you will go home with the girl tonight!"

I just stood there with a smile. "You're a pretty good friend Senator; thank you very much."

He jokingly replied, "Well, you know what Huey Long always said, if you have a friend then you have a vote." Then he just smiled with a big grin and said. "Come on were wasting time Romeo." With that said, I was off to prove my love for Kelly or make the biggest ass out of myself, at that point it could have gone either way.

It didn't take us that long to get across town to Kelly's apartment building. As the senator promised there was a crowd blocking the street that the building was in front of. It looked more like a protest rally than a sympathetic crowd. I asked the senator how he got so many people there in one place so quickly. He just told me his staff went to every gay hangout nearby and told them there was a rally for gay rights and a gay couple was getting married in public. According to the Senator, gays would always turn out for a good party. That wasn't necessarily true and he was often unaware and misinformed, which made him a perfect politician.

I looked at the senator and said. "But, I'm not gay and the crowd they won't get get hostile once they know what's going on."

"Don't worry about it...once they see you making a fool of yourself and professing your love, they'll all be emotional and think it's cute; you'll probably get a few numbers too."

I looked at him with a disgruntled look. "Thank you, that's very comforting to know, but let's hope I get the girl, because the last thing I need is guys asking me out. Oh, by the way it's nice to know you still a staunch conservative with misguided notions about homosexuals."

"Hey, we all have an image we have to maintain, especially when it comes to politics."

The pilot landed the helicopter on the building across the from Kelly's apartment building. The crowd was already in a frenzy, especially when the cross-dressers got there; if nothing else by the time I arrived, that street was turning into one hell of a party. People in the apartment complex were starting to look out their windows at the crowd. Not, Kelly though. We got to the very center of the street after I had tried to get inside the apartment building, but couldn't because she wouldn't buzz me in.

With the senator standing next to me and with the crowd yelling, I asked him "Well, what should I do now, I mean, how do I get her attention?"
The senator replied back. "Hey, do I have to figure everything out, get creative."

Right when he finished his sentence I had an idea; I would get the crowd to chant a certain phrase until she came to her window. We got the entire crowd to shout her name until she came to her window. With almost a thousand people in front of the building she was bound to hear us. The crowd of mostly gay couples, cross-dressers, drag queens, and anybody who was just on the sidewalks, walking down the street started to shout, "Kelly." It sounded more like a sporting event or a political rally. After a few minutes of this, she finally heard what they were saying and came to the window to see what was really going on. When she opened up her window and looked out, she saw me immediately at the base of the crowd,

And when the crowd finally started to quiet down I shouted three stories up to her. "Kelly. Don't leave tonight... I love you and I don't want you to go."

Using all the courage I could find, I tried to convince Kelly to stay. With a puzzled look, Kelly shouted down to me. "Blake what is all this and who are all these people?"

I shouted back "Please don't leave because I can't live without you."

"Why should I stay?"

I said to her. "What do you mean, I just told you why you should stay; I love you with all my heart."

"Blake, we've been through this...that's not enough."

I started to shout a smart-ass comment to her and then looked over at the Senator. He just shrugged his shoulders and shook his head as if to say he didn't know what to do next. There's no rule book or plan for this sort of thing. You just have to wing it and hope that it works out.

At that moment I saw an electrical lift with maintenance workers on it who had been painting part of the apartment building. I ran over and convinced them to give me a ride up to the third floor and Kelly's window. They were to happy oblige me and lifted me up to her. The maintenance guy who rode up with me stood there grinning at me. This was highly entertaining for them. I was still a little scared, but knew, that I had to swallow my pride and speak from the heart. I had to take a leap of faith   It didn't matter who was down there below, or up, on the life with me, or even if Kelly said "no." I had to try...one last try before it was too late.

This was it, in front of a huge crowd of alternative life-stylers and a maintenance worker and like some sappy romantic movie, I let the romance of it all, inspire me. I looked at her straight in the eye and said. "You don't make things easy do you because for you, never is not good enough?"

She just smiled at me and waited for me to finish what I was saying. "Look, Kelly I am not a big fan of marriage, but I want to spend the rest of my life with you. It's true, I'm terrified that I might end up like my parents and fail at it, but I am willing to take that chance, if it means, I get to spend my life with you. I know you think that I should want marriage and not just willing to do it, but it doesn't work that way."

I paused, waiting for her to say something. She didn't. Somehow, she knew, I had more to say so she didn't interrupt, My heart was doing the talking now. "I don't want to know what life is without you. You are the last person I want to talk to before I fall asleep and the first person I want to see when I wake up. I am more terrified of having to live a life without you than being married. You can get on that plane and we will go on with our lives, but I am here, because I choose to take that chance on you and me. If there is any choice that has to be made about marriage, or living with our fears, or a life together then I choose you and me. I don't want to marry you because I want to be in a marriage...I want to marry you because I want to spend the rest of my life with you. I don't know what else to say and I don't know how many times I need to say what I've been saying, but I love you with everything I am, You are the one that makes the difference in my life. You are the only one I could ever want. I don't have a ring and I should, but I'm asking you...marry me...don't go...marry me."

Kelly just smiled as a tear ran down her face. She said. "That's all I wanted to hear from you, even if it was just once and your stubbornness never allows you to say something like that again; Blake I love you and always have and will never stop. You make the difference in my life too, and there is no one else I would rather spend my life with too. If you wanted to marry, I just wanted you to do for the right reasons, not just saying it because you want me to go."

I started to cry. Yeah, it's true, I started to cry too. I replied. "I know...I guess, I didn't understand what you were trying to say, but I do now and you were right. So I ask again...marry me!"

The sun started to break from the clouds and shine as if it was only on us. Maybe God was shining a spotlight on us. I wish that I could say it had to do with the moment and it probably didn't, but I like to think it did anyway. Kelly smiled that beautiful smile she's always had. She kissed me and said. "How about that for an answer.

I replied. "That's a great answer."

She laughed, "It's about time you came around I was really getting worried about you." Then she kissed me again softly and passionately like two people who had been apart for years.

The crowd was roaring in excitement and even the maintenance worker shed a tear or two, he tried to hide it, but I saw it. Kelly looked at me again and asked, "Now, are you going to tell me who all these people are?"

Smiling, I replied back to her. "I honestly don't know; it was just a crowd put together to help convince you to stay."

Kelly just grinned. "You did all this just to get me to stay?"

"Yes, with a little help, of course; I didn't know what I was going to do if you said "no" so the crowd was here to help convince you to say "yes'."

"Wow, good call, I like big gestures... you are finally beginning to learn the way to my heart."

"Good, I'm glad my understanding of your heart is getting better because I can't take going through the motions with you anymore. You know I always tried to be a good student. " And then I brought her onto the lift and kissed her long and slow, hoping to just be lost within the moment. John Wayne would have been proud of me, I think! We couldn't help it, we just wanted to keep on kissing. I am constantly reminded when I look at her how much I have always wanted to spend the rest of my life with her. And a how much I need her. It may be an understatement at this point,

but I am very thankful for the blessing that
is Kelly.

9

As I got another cup of coffee, I thought to myself everything that had happened back then. My life is the better with her in it and hopefully she still feels the same about me. The fact she is still with me is evidence enough. Yes, it was a happy ending to a long journey and it felt just like something out of a movie. I tend not to believe in stuff like that, but in truth that's the way it really happened.

As it turned out Kelly and I decided the best thing to do was to get married in San Diego. Figured it was best to get married because the alternative was a lot worse. I don't mean to make it sound like a consolation prize; it was the best thing that could have ever happened. And I don't regret a thing. She had already made plans to go to San Diego so we went, got married, and had a honeymoon there since she had to find a replacement job anyway. Every day with her since has only gotten better, even though we've had a few surprises along the way. But that night...the night she said "yes," we had one hell of a block party celebrating our union. Turned out to be the best wedding party since our ceremony was a small affair,

I Looked at Joe, who was sitting across the table and still wide awake. He was still hanging onto every word I said. I smiled. "Well, that's it, this is my love story and how I found happiness. It was a long emotional journey for us, but one that had a happy ending. I don't know what would have happened if she hadn't come to her window; I definitely wouldn't be sitting here at 5:30am telling you this story."

Joe just started laughing. "I admit, I've never heard a story like that and never seen more examples of what not to do when you're trying to find love. I guess it's true you never know what you might do when you're in love, no matter how stupid it might be."

I had to laugh because everything about this was humorous. I replied back. "I know the story sounds very melodramatic and a little exaggerated, but everything I told you is true and that's exactly how it happened. It's amazing how human beings act when dealing with love and the stupid things we do to try to achieve it. There are too many games we go through and too much drama we bring upon ourselves when we are too afraid or insecure to say how we truly feel about people. As you can see that's what happened to me and a lot of it could have been avoided if I had just been honest from the start. Although, I do think it worked out quite nicely for me and it makes my story more romantic for the female listeners. And it made one hell of a

Thank Full note down at the station. The best one if you ask me, but I admit...I'm biased."

Joe nodded in agreement. "That was definitely worth hearing over pancakes and alcohol. It's a good story."

Before we left I had one final thing to say, even to Steve, who had the story many times and despite being a part of it. I looked at Joe. "Take what you want from the story and believe me one shouldn't be that stupid as I demonstrated so expertly. Although, sometimes it is worth it and it makes you a better person in the long run because of the journey or at least that is what I keep telling myself. I can't tell you what you should do with your girlfriend, Joe; you will have to figure that out on your own and hopefully this story will help you. That's probably the only advice I can really give you. "

We left the IHOP at dawn. As we were leaving, the sun peaked over the mountains. Radiant, I thought, looking for my car. It was the promise of a new day. It had one more thing to say to Joe, something profound. "There's one more piece advice I can give about your relationship; if you truly love your girlfriend then go home and give her a long, deep, slow kiss that last for days and says everything that's needs to be said. Sometimes we have to show how we feel without the words and put meaning behind our actions. If you love her whether you want to get or married or not, you should never let her pass through your life without telling or showing her what she has meant to you."

I got in my car and headed home to my beautiful wife. She was all that I thought about on my way home. My journey with Kelly was very hard and in the beginning I took more from her than I gave. I was not always fair to her. I didn't always give what she really needed from me, and we were both to blame for a lot of the bad things that happened between us even though I blame myself for all of it. I haven't always loved her the way I should, but I spend every day trying to make her happy because she makes me happy. There's isn't just one reason why I love her because it's a million things wrapped up in one, but even though it's hard sometimes, I am a better person with her in my life. I've probably said that before, but it's worth reminding. It's the main reason I stay. Couldn't imagine life without her! It's also what makes being with her, worth it.

I arrived home about 6:00am and Kelly was just getting up to start the coffee. It was hard for her to move around being eight months pregnant, but she managed slowly. Even then when she first rises out of bed and looks twice her size, Kelly was still serene. She kissed me good morning and wondered where I had been all night. I told her that I was telling another friend our story.

She casually laughed and said. "You just love telling that story and can't ever pass up an opportunity to do so even if it takes all night."

Smiling, I replied back to her. "It is the best story that I know."

She just smiled that beautiful smile. That same smile she always had, every day. It told me how happy she was that I came after her that time and that she was happy she came to the window. She turned around and walked into the kitchen and as she passed through the sunlight coming through the window while glowing like a rose in full bloom. It was one more reminder that I had made the right choice.

I went to our bedroom to get changed. I was happy, but it didn't last. All of a sudden, I had crashing dishes and Kelly scream in pain. There were pits in my stomach as I rushed to the kitchen and found her on the floor. It looked as if her water had broken, but she sat in a pool of blood. Something was horribly wrong. You didn't have to know anything about biology or anatomy to know that the pool of blood coming from her uterus was bad. I called an ambulance. They got to our house pretty quick and rushed us to the hospital. It was scarier not knowing what was going on. The paramedics didn't have an answer either, which made it the longest ride of my life.

When we got to the hospital, Kelly was immediately wheeled into one of the emergency rooms. I wasn't allowed to go in and told to go to a waiting room. They didn't need me in there, but I could hear her screams. I waited for what seemed like hours, pacing in the waiting room back and forth because I just couldn't sit still. Sitting still would be like admitting defeat in some strange way. I was only there for less than an hour before a doctor came out. The look on his face told me immediately that it was bad news. He didn't have a good poker face. It wasn't good news. There was a uterine rupture and Kelly started hemorrhaging blood. She was dead. They tried to save her, according to the doctor, but it happened so fast that they couldn't do anything for her. They didn't even know at this point, what caused it.

When I heard the news I fell to my knees. I didn't want to believe it. No, it couldn't possibly be true. And worse of all, I hadn't even asked about the baby yet. The doctor told me as he helped me to my feet that the baby was fine. They had performed a C-Section and though the baby was born premature, she was perfectly healthy. I heard the heard the words come out of the doctor's mouth and replied. "A girl, I have a baby girl." The doctor smiled and said "yes." A nurse took me to the nursery. When we got there, I couldn't go in yet. I could only stand outside the window, but the blinds were closed. Finally a nurse opened them and there she was, my daughter. I was happy to see her, but my tears were for both joy and sorrow. Everything had happened fast and I was still numb over the whole thing. But there was this sinking feeling that I could not ignore. I was already missing Kelly.

10

I opened my eyes. Everything moved fast. Scenes were traveling at the speed of the light in my head as I saw the future of what could be. I admit, it scared the hell out of me... all of it. And as I sat on the small bench trying to convince myself to go find her and talk to her again, I kept debating whether I should. Would it make any difference at all, if I already knew the future? It was like opening your presents on Christmas when you already knew what they were. There weren't any surprises. But there I sat, on a bench, not wanting to make a choice so I could stay in the same moment that seemed safe and secure from my lingering self-doubt.

Last night had been one of the best nights of life. It felt like fate had brought me here. Maybe it God, I don't know. But some kind of powerful cosmic brought me here so I could meet her. This was no ordinary event...that much I was sure. Finally, I spoke out loud. "I may not be able to see you, but I know you're there."

Then I heard the voice. "Blake, I've always been here. I'm here when you need me."

The voice had always felt so familiar, like I had known it all my life. And I had always felt at peace when I heard the voice. I didn't know what to say, but I muttered the words, "Thank You."

The Voice replied. "What can I help you with?"

"I don't know what to do?"

"About the girl, you met last night?"

I smiled just thinking of her. "Yes...I want to talk to her again, but..."

"But what," the voice interrupted. "Go talk to her."

"It's not that simple. What if I already know what's going to happen? What if I know the outcome of it all and it doesn't end well."

The Voice chuckled. "You think because you've seen the future, you know how this ends?"

"Yes and it's scary."

"It's one possible future, doesn't mean it's written in stone. There are so many choices you can make that will affect the outcome."

I looked over at the Voice. While I couldn't really make out the face, it was familiar, like I had seen it many times before. But the face wasn't something that stood out, it didn't have any distinguishable features. However, it was comforting to see the face. I replied. "I know what I saw, the future was plain as day."

"You have the gift of insight, not seeing the absolute future. Your insight is only there to guide you in your choices, not make them for you."

"But it felt so real."

"Our worst fears can make what we see as the future seem real. But how worse could it be if you never talked to her again. Wouldn't that be the bigger tragedy?"

I had a look of confusion. "Then how do I know what's real?"

"You don't...you're not supposed to when it comes to seeing the future, but you can make your own future and that's where the gift of insight helps."

"So what I saw doesn't necessarily happen."

"Maybe...maybe not."

"That's vague."

The Voice smiled. "You're forgetting something. The best part of the journey is every moment you could spend with her...no matter how long or how short they are.   Your happiness is found in those moments and when they're added together...it could be one hell of life...a life worth living."

"And if it ends in tragedy?"

"It doesn't take away from the moments you have leading up to the tragedy. All things end, no stopping it, but do you have the courage to live until the end does come!"

I smiled. The Voice's words were comforting. I couldn't explain it, but somehow they were. I only had one question for the Voice. "Are you my guardian angel?"

The Voice softly laughed. "I've been called that before, but I've been called many things...your inner voice, your conscience...even God. The truth is...I am whatever you need me to be to help you navigate this wretched life. I am here to make things easier for you. Call me whatever you want."

I smiled until I couldn't see or hear the Voice anymore. It was just me on the bench now. I had debated with myself for long enough. There was a flower garden near me filled with all sorts of beautiful flowers. The campus was filled with these flower gardens to help make it more beautiful, especially during the spring and summer before winter came and changed everything to gray. I found a pinkish reddish rose with hints of white on the petals. It was unique. It was stunning. I picked it from the garden, even though I probably wasn't supposed to. If I was going to make a fool of myself, I might as well bring flowers.

Her dorm room wasn't hard to find. It was the one with these huge bay windows and you could usually find students sitting on the window sills reading or drinking coffee. Instead of going inside the dorm and looking for her, I asked another student where her window was. She pointed it out and as luck would have it, it was on the first floor. I found the window and it was partially cracked open. Hoping that she was there, I walked up and knocked on it. It wasn't uncommon for guys to do that when looking for girls at the dorm because of the bay windows that seem to welcome visitors.

She was there and came to the window. As she opened it, I saw that beautiful smile that was easy to get lost in. Almost did for a moment. She was happy to see me and said. "Wow, you found me."

I smiled back. "I did. I wanted to see you again after spending such a wonderful night talking with you. Couldn't stop thinking about you."

She looked down at the rose. "Is that for me?"

"Yes. I saw it and thought of you. So I made it my mission today to find you, Kelly." It sounded like a cheap romantic line, but far from it because it was the truth. And the best romantic lines are the most truthful.

Kelly added an infectious laugh to compliment her beautiful smile. Then she replied.   "I'm glad you found me."

~ The End ~